"This is the p[...] the man with th[...] that came to his toes.

"But it's just a pile of rocks," Tam said. "This can't be Faery."

Pix was grizzling and grunting, waving her hands about and kicking her feet in the air, rocking the pram so wildly that Tam thought she would fall out of it any minute.

"See that crack between those big pointed rocks?" said Great-grandpa.

Tam nodded.

"That's the green passage. You have to go through there."

YOUNG CORGI BOOKS

Young Corgi books are perfect when you are looking for great books to read on your own. They are full of exciting stories and entertaining pictures. There are funny books, scary books, spine-tingling stories and mysterious ones. Whatever your interests you'll find something in Young Corgi to suit you: from families to football, from ponies to ghosts. The books are written by some of the most famous and popular of today's children's authors, and by some of the best new talents, too.

Whether you read one chapter a night, or devour the whole book in one sitting, you'll love Young Corgi - books to get your teeth into!

Other Young Corgi books to get your teeth into:
Tilly Mint Tales by Berlie Doherty
Dogspell by Helen Dunwoodie
Titus Rules OK! by Dick King-Smith

www.berliedoherty.com

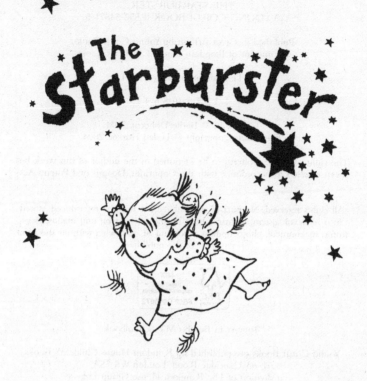

The Starburster

Berlie Doherty

Illustrated by Lesley Harker

YOUNG CORGI

For Tim, Verena and Baby

THE STARBURSTER
A YOUNG CORGI BOOK 0 552 54871 5

Published in Great Britain by Young Corgi Books,
an imprint of Random House Children's Books

This edition published 2004

1 3 5 7 9 10 8 6 4 2

MIX
Paper from
responsible sources
FSC
www.fsc.org   FSC® C018072

Typeset in Bembo MT Schoolbook

Young Corgi Books are published by Random House Children's Books,
61–63 Uxbridge Road, London W5 5SA,
a division of The Random House Group Ltd,
in Australia by Random House Australia (Pty) Ltd,
20 Alfred Street, Milsons Point, Sydney, NSW 2061, Australia,
in New Zealand by Random House New Zealand Ltd,
18 Poland Road, Glenfield, Auckland 10, New Zealand,
and in South Africa by Random House (Pty) Ltd,
Endulini, 5A Jubilee Road, Parktown 2193, South Africa

THE RANDOM HOUSE GROUP Limited Reg. No. 954009
www.kidsatrandomhouse.co.uk

A CIP catalogue record for this book is available from the British Library.

Printed and bound in Great Britain by Clays Ltd, St Ives PLC

Contents

Blue 01

Sapphire Stars 08

The Changeling 13

Pixillated 18

"Only You Can Do It, Tam" 23

Something of Silver and
   Something of Velvet 29

Through the Green Passage 35

Prince Tamlin 39

Go Wisely, Go Bravely 47

The Sapphire Lake 50

The Fairy Castle 57

The Food of Fairies 64

The Starburster Is Stolen 71

Tanta 75

The Baby Glade 82

Keekwee Baba 87

The Secret Tower 91

Blue Is Found 96

The King of the Fairies 101

The Starburster 107

Home 113

Blue

On the day Tam's baby sister was born, he painted his finger blue.

"Look at that boy with the blue finger," some people said. "He must be very special."

One of these people was his great-grandpa Toby. He winked at Tam and said, "You must be very special. Your little sister will be proud of you one day."

Other people said, "Look at that boy with the blue finger. He must be very silly."

One of these people was Dad. "Don't be silly, Tam," he said. "You don't want your little sister to be scared of you, do you?" He made Tam wash the paint off and took him to the hospital to see Mum and the baby. Mum was in bed and the baby cried all the time and Tam wished he still had his blue finger.

On the day the baby was brought home from hospital Tam hid in the bathroom. The baby cried all the time when she wasn't drinking milk from Mum. Tam decided to make her a drink of her own. He squeezed some toothpaste into a jug of warm water and stirred it round with the end of his toothbrush, then carried it carefully downstairs.

"My word, she'll enjoy that," Great-grandpa Toby said.

But Dad took one sniff at it and poured it down the sink.

"Would you like to hold Baby for a bit?" Mum said.

"No," said Tam, and ran up to his room. "I wish that baby would go away!" he shouted.

Great-grandpa followed him up to his room. "I've got a present for you, Tam," he said. "It's my most special thing." He went into his room and came back with a yellow sock in his hand.

"A sock?" said Tam.

"Look inside it."

Tam put his hand in the sock and pulled out a little tube.

"Hold it up to your eye, and swizzle it round," said Great-grandpa. "What do you see?"

It was the most marvellous thing. When Tam looked through it, he could see eight Great-grandpas all cut into little pieces. He couldn't stop giggling. When he turned it towards the bed, he could see eight beds all topsy-turvy, and all kinds of patterns of colours. He had eight new red dressing gowns, and they swayed and billowed like princes' cloaks. And when he looked out of the window, he could see eight gardens in tiny slices of colour, as brilliant as rainbows.

"It's called a kaleidoscope," said Great-grandpa. "But I call it a starburster. Yes, starburster's a good name for it."

"Can I really keep it?" Tam asked. He couldn't stop looking at things and twisting the tube round to make them glow and splinter and swirl with colours. It really did look as if stars were bursting open inside it.

"Of course you can. Shall we go down and look at Baby through it?"

Baby was asleep when they went downstairs. Tam looked through the kaleidoscope at her and twisted it this way and that, so there were eight pink blobs and sixteen fisty hands and sixteen stubby feet.

"Would you like to hold her?" Dad said.

"No thank you," said Tam, peering at him through the kaleidoscope. "You've broken into lots of pieces."

"What shall we call her?" Mum asked.

"Your faces are like balloons," Tam giggled, peering at Mum. "And all your noses are all over the place."

"My word, I bet you'll look funny, holding the baby," Great-grandpa said. "Can I have a look?"

So Tam gave Great-grandpa the starburster and sat next to Mum on the settee, and Mum put the baby into his arms. Tam couldn't believe how soft she was, and how light and warm and sweet-smelling, and how quiet and still and gentle, and how peaceful her breathing was. Her hands fluttered open like butterflies and her fingers wrapped themselves round his thumb. Tam daren't move in case he dropped her. He hardly dared breathe. Then, for a second, her eyes opened. They were as blue as the sky. She stared right at Tam.

"What do you think of her?" Mum said.

"I love her." Tam's voice was just a whisper. "Can we call her Blue?"

Sapphire Stars

When Tam wasn't cuddling Blue, he
was playing with his starburster. He
looked at everything through it, and
everything looked strange and
wonderful. But the best thing of all was
looking at the stars. They shone and
sparkled and danced through the
starburster as though they were birds
made of diamonds. Dad had to keep
coming up to Tam's room and putting
the starburster back in its yellow sock
so Tam would go to sleep.

"I don't know which I love best,"
Tam said. "My starburster or Blue."

Then, one night, something awful
happened. Blue was stolen.

The night started off very well. Tam was looking through his starburster and he noticed that some of the stars seemed to be swarming like bees. They seemed to be coming towards the house. They seemed to be brilliant blue.

He shouted to Great-grandpa, and he woke up at once and came hurrying into Tam's room.

"My word, they're like sapphires," Great-grandpa said, twisting the kaleidoscope excitedly.

"What's a sapphire?" Tam asked.

"It's a precious stone. It's very rare. A jewel. And it's blue."

"But why have the stars turned into sapphires?" Tam asked.

"My word, I don't know everything!" Great-grandpa said. "Better go to sleep now, Tam."

And Tam did try to go to sleep, but a strange sound kept waking him up. It was like the sound of tiny wings beating, like hundreds of moths fluttering against the window.

At last he drifted off to sleep, and in no time at all he was woken up by the sound of Blue crying. Then the crying turned to screaming. He put his fingers in his ears and tried to block the noise out. "That's the trouble with babies," he said to himself. "They never stop crying."

The screaming turned to a wailing that was so high-pitched he thought his ears would break. It was the worst sound Blue had ever made. In fact it didn't sound like Blue at all. Mum was shouting now, and Dad was shouting, and then Mum started crying too. Then the high-pitched sound turned into a howl like a dog, and Tam sat up and jumped out of bed. What *was* the matter with her? The howling suddenly turned into shrieks of laughing. But Blue never laughed like that. She was far too young yet to do anything but gurgle and chuckle.

Tam ran into Blue's room. They were all in there – Mum, Dad and Great-grandpa – all gathered round the baby's cot and staring into it. No one was making any attempt to pick her up.

"Blue, Blue, what's the matter?" Tam shouted. He ran to the cot and stared down at the ugliest baby he had ever seen. It had pointed ears and a tippety nose and a screwed-up cross little face.

"What's happened?" Tam asked. "Where's Blue?"

Mum burst into tears. "Blue's been stolen," she sobbed. "And this little goblin thing's been left in her place."

The Changeling

Tam couldn't take his eyes off the goblin thing. It really was very ugly. But its eyes were as brilliant as blue jewels.

"Sapphires," Tam whispered to Great-grandpa. "Just like those stars we saw."

"What did you say?" Dad asked.

Great-grandpa looked worried.

"The stars were whizzing about last night, weren't they, Great-grandpa? They were deep, deep blue, just like her eyes," said Tam. "And things were flying and fluttering right round the house."

Dad sat down with his head in his hands. "Why didn't you tell me? You silly old man!"

"You were asleep," Great-grandpa muttered. "Anyway, it was nothing, it was nothing."

"What's all that got to do with this ugly thing in Blue's cot?" Mum demanded. "And where is Blue anyway? Where's my baby?"

"Ask Grandpa," Dad said. "He reckons he knows about such things."

Great-grandpa Toby took out his hankie and blew his nose loudly. "Yes, I think I do know. I think this baby is a changeling."

Mum gasped and started crying again.

Tam glared at the baby. She pulled a
face at him and he pulled one back,
his best one, with his eyes rolled up
and his lips curled back like sausages.
Instead of crying, the baby giggled and
tried to copy him.

"My word," said Great-grandpa, "I've never heard a little baby laugh like that before. It really must be a changeling."

"What's a changeling?" Tam asked.

"A changeling is a fairy child," said Great-grandpa.

"I've heard of this happening," Mum sobbed. "The fairies come and steal a mortal baby and leave a nasty little goblinny thing in its place. I'll never see my baby again!"

The changeling baby stopped pulling faces at Tam and smiled sweetly at him instead. She held out her arms as if she wanted him to pick her up.

"She's really, really ugly," said Tam.

Mum burst into tears again and ran out of the room, and Dad ran after her. Great-grandpa sighed deeply and sat on the chair. The changeling baby gurgled up at Tam.

"She likes you," Great-grandpa said.

"Well I don't like her. I'd rather have Blue back, any day." Tam tried not to catch the goblin-thing's eyes, but she was smiling her crooked smile at him and staring straight at him with her dazzling blue eyes. It made him feel very strange. He could hardly take his eyes off her.

"She's bewitching you," Great-grandpa said.

"No she's not," said Tam. "I'm not going to look at her."

But as soon as he said it, he wanted to look at her again. He went to bed, but all he wanted to do then was to go back to the changeling's room and peer round the door at her. Maybe what Great-grandpa had said was true. Maybe she *had* bewitched him.

Pixillated

Mum and Dad refused to go near the changeling, but Tam was worried that she might be hungry. He took her some cornflakes and she scowled at him. He took her a bottle of milk and she crossed her eyes.

"She seems all right," said Great-grandpa. "And I don't suppose she'd eat mortal food anyway."

When no one was looking except Tam, the baby stared at a vase of roses till all the flowers flew across the room and landed in her cot.

She gobbled them up greedily, thorns and all. Then she lay back, burping loudly.

"Can I carry her into the garden?" Tam asked Mum. "I think she likes flowers."

"Just leave her alone," Mum said. "Try to forget she's here."

But how could they forget? The changeling shrieked and howled whenever Tam wasn't in her room. As soon as he went in, she stopped. They played the faces game for hours.

"My word, better not go out when the wind's blowing," Great-grandpa said. "Soon as it stops, your face will stick like that."

"It's not my fault," said Tam. "She's making me do it. It's her eyes."

She could do other things with her eyes. She could make all kinds of things happen. When she stared at the cupboard, the doors flew open and all the things in it tumbled out in a mess on the floor. Then she just chuckled and closed her eyes and went to sleep, and nobody but Tam knew it was anything to do with her.

"Did you make that mess?" Mum demanded.

"No, it was the baby," Tam said.

"Don't be silly. Babies can't climb out of their cots and open doors," Mum said. "Not even goblinny things like this one." But she glared at the sleeping baby all the same.

If the baby stared at the clock, the cuckoo popped in and out of its door so wildly that it drove everybody mad with its cuckooing. Nobody saw her do

it except Tam. In
the end Dad took
the clock off the
wall and put it
in the bin.

CUCKOO!

They could hear it cuckooing to itself
out in the yard.

"Cuckoo," sang the goblin baby.
"Cuckoo."

"Shut UP!" shouted Mum.

The baby stared at the window and
the glass shattered like stars.

"My word, this house is pixillated all
right," Great-grandpa chuckled. "I
haven't had such fun for years."

"What's pixillated?" Tam asked.

"Bewitched, enchanted, full of
mischief," Dad said.

Tam leaned over the baby's cot and she blew bubbles at him.

"It's you, isn't it?" Tam whispered. "Pixillating everything, that's what you're doing. I think we should call you Pix."

And the baby smiled at him so sweetly that he actually smiled back. He just couldn't help it.

Great-grandpa came and stood next to him. "My word, you mustn't let her charm you," he said. "Your poor mum's very upset. That baby has to go."

"Go where?"

"Where she belongs," Great-grandpa whispered. "Faery, that's where she comes from. The land of the fairies. Someone's got to take her back there, Tam."

"Only You Can Do It, Tam"

As soon as Mum and Dad had gone out of the room he said it again, only louder, so Tam couldn't pretend he hadn't heard him.

"Someone has to take her to Faery, give her back to the king of the fairies, find Blue and bring her home."

"I suppose so," Tam agreed.

"And there's only you can do it, Tam. My word, you're a brave boy."

"Me? But I can't do that! I'm only nine years old!"

"Exactly," Great-grandpa Toby agreed. "That's why you have to do it."

"But I don't even know how to get there."

"I know the way in," Great-grandpa said. "It's called the green passage."

"How do you know that?"

"Because I once met someone who'd actually been there! He was a very old man, but when he went in, he was just a little boy, like you. And when he came out, he was an old, old man with a beard down to his toes. He'd been there a hundred years, and it just seemed like a day, he said."

"Great-grandpa, I'm not going."

"He told me how to get there, if I ever wanted to go. I never dared. I wasn't brave enough. But I used to go and sit by the green passage and wait in case any fairies came out. I thought I saw the king of the fairies himself, at that very spot, when I was looking through my starburster. Just for a second, I think I saw him, all dressed in green, with hair like dandelion fluff. I think he wanted my starburster, but he wasn't having it. That was ninety years ago." He opened his eyes wide with surprise. "Ninety years!"

"I don't want to go, Great-grandpa."

"You have to take something of your own that's silver and something of your own that's velvet, or you'll never get past the guardian, that's what the old man told me."

Tam sighed with relief. "Well, I can't do it. I haven't got anything of silver, and I haven't got anything of velvet."

Great-grandpa shook his head. "I think you have, Tam. I'm sure you have. And you have to give your favourite thing of all to the king of the fairies."

"My favourite thing? That's not fair!"

"If he gives you Blue back, that's fair, isn't it?"

Tam nodded sadly. He'd almost forgotten about Blue, he'd got so used to Pix.

"You have a think, and I'll have a lie-down," said Great-grandpa. He yawned noisily. "There's something else you have to do, only I can't remember what it is. If you don't do it, you won't come back for a hundred years, like that old man I met. Only I can't remember what it is." He went off to his own room to lie down.

"I really don't want to go!" Tam called after him.

Pix was making her favourite little high-pitched yelping noises. The moon was shining into her cot and she was holding out her hands to it as if she was trying to pull herself up onto its beams. Tam went to his own bedroom. Mum and Dad would be trying to sleep, he knew, but Pix would be keeping them awake, like she always did. He tried to sleep himself but it was impossible. Her screeches were getting louder. He went back to her room and put his hand through the bars of her cot, and she grabbed hold of his fingers.

"What's the matter, Pix?" he asked. "Do you want to go home?"

As soon as he said that, she stopped crying. And straight away she fell asleep, smiling.

Great-grandpa hurried into the room with his felt slippers flapping and his eyes shining. "I've just remembered what that other thing was! If you don't want to stay in Faery for a hundred years, you have to get there before the stroke of noon on midsummer's day. That's tomorrow, Tam!"

Something of Silver and Something of Velvet

Tam didn't sleep a wink that night. He lifted Pix out of her cot and carried her into his room and put her on his bed. Then he searched through his toys to see if he had something of silver and something of velvet to take. He knew what his favourite thing was, of course. He had no doubt about that, but he wasn't at all happy about giving it to the king of the fairies.

Great-grandpa fussed round the room, clapping his hands and saying, "My word, I can't believe it! Young Tam's going to Faery!"

Tam sat back on his heels. "I don't want to go. But I'm going to rescue Blue," he said, trying to make himself feel brave and happy about it.

"Something velvet and something silver," Great-grandpa reminded him. "Be quick. Oh, I've remembered something else! The silver thing has to be sharp."

"Something silver and sharp," Tam said, gazing round at his pile of things. "Like a . . . "

"Sword!" they both said together, and Pix woke up and stared at the cupboard, and out fell Tam's toy sword. She closed her eyes and chuckled.

"But it isn't sharp at all, because it's only plastic," Tam said. "And it isn't really silver. It's only grey paint."

"Never mind," said Great-grandpa. "It'll do. Something velvet now."

They looked hopelessly round the room.

"Cotton curtains," muttered Great-grandpa. "They're no use. Anyway, they're your mum's. It has to be something of yours."

They stared at the window. Dawn was coming. If they didn't find something soon, it would be too late. Pix started crying, opened her eyes again and glared at the door. And there it was. It just flew off the hook where it always hung, and draped itself round Tam's shoulders.

"My red dressing gown!" he said.
"With its velvet collar!" He stroked the
collar. How he loved the feel of it,
rough one way, smooth the other, just
like a cat's nose.

Great-grandpa took it off Tam's
shoulders and rolled it up. He carried it
downstairs and put it at the bottom of
Pix's pram, then he came back up for

Pix and carried her down. Tam followed with the sword and put it carefully in the pram across Pix's blankets. He couldn't help feeling a surge of excitement as he laid it there. His hand stretched across to touch it.

"Use it carefully," Great-grandpa warned.

"Use it?" said Tam, suddenly scared. "How do I use it?"

"I'm sure the guardian will give you instructions," Great-grandpa said. "There's bound to be Faery rules. They can't just let anyone wander round and do what they like there, can they? Now, Tam, fetch the favourite thing."

Pix chuckled gleefully.

"I wish I didn't have to," said Tam.

"I know," said Great-grandpa.

Tam went back to his room and opened the drawer by the bed. He took out the starburster in its yellow sock. He had a lump in his throat. He felt sadder than he had ever felt before. He carried it downstairs and put it in the pram without saying anything, and Great-grandpa didn't say anything either.

But an amazing thing happened then. The changeling baby stretched out her hands as if she wanted to touch it. Then she nodded her head and smiled, just as if she understood exactly what was going on.

Through the Green Passage

They left the house just as the sun was pushing above the rooftops. All the air seemed to be golden that morning. They didn't wake Mum and Dad, though Tam was longing to tell them that he was going to find baby Blue and bring her home again. But he knew Mum would worry and fuss and cry, and that would never do. Tam would never be able to leave if she did that. And Dad would insist on coming with him, and that would never do either. Dad wasn't a little boy.

So he and Great-grandpa and Pix in her pram went out of the house as quietly as they could, down the street and through the park and across the river and towards the boulders, and at last Great-grandpa stopped.

"This is the place. This is where I met the man with the long white beard that came to his toes."

"But it's just a pile of rocks," Tam said. "This can't be Faery."

Pix was grizzling and grunting, waving her hands about and kicking her feet in the air, rocking the pram so wildly that Tam thought she would fall out of it any minute.

"See that crack between those big pointed rocks?" said Great-grandpa.

Tam nodded.

"That's the green passage. You have to go through there." He bent down and kissed Tam. "My word, you're a brave boy."

Tam's courage was draining away. He didn't feel a bit brave. He wanted to go back home and have a nice breakfast of toast and marmalade instead of going to Faery.

"I don't really want to . . ." he began.

"I'm proud of you," Great-grandpa said.

So Tam gripped the handle of Pix's pram and walked forward towards the crack. He turned round, and Great-grandpa nodded and waved and blew him a kiss. He turned back, and the two great boulders began to roll apart, and the narrow crack opened out to a passage that was as green as summer leaves. Tam took two more steps, then three, then seven, and he was inside the passage. He took two more, and the two great boulders rolled together again like huge doors closing behind him.

Prince Tamlin

It was completely dark now, and completely silent. Tam stood very still, and he and Pix both held their breath.

Something was happening. Tam could hear the sound of shuffling feet, and they were getting closer, closer. They stopped in front of Pix's pram. Now Tam could hear the sound of someone breathing.

Suddenly there was a flash like blue lightning and the passage was lit by a flickering light. Standing in front of Tam was a skinny old man with a green beard and long green hair. He stared at Tam, and Tam stared back at him, too afraid to speak.

The old man pointed a bony finger
at him and said, "Splix."

"Splix?" Tam said
back.

"Who? Splix! Who?"
the man asked,
stamping his foot.

"Who? Tam, I'm Tam.
Are you – are you the
king of the fairies?"

"Sploof!" the skinny
man growled. "Not king!
Look-after. I look after."

"Oh! Are you a sort of
guardian?"

"All of 'em's look
after." The skinny man
swung his arms and the
floor of the passage lit up.
Men were lying all
around them, still as
stones. "Faery soldiers,"
he whispered.

"Are they all dead?" Tam asked.

"Sploof!" the old man said again. "Slumber. Hinx hundert year-in year-out." He held up ten fingers.

"Ten hundred! They've been asleep for ten hundred years. A thousand years?"

Look-after grinned pointed green teeth at him.

"Can't they ever wake up?"

At that moment Pix woke up from her own deep sleep and began to whimper, and at the sound of the baby crying the sleeping soldiers turned over onto their backs.

"Whishht! Wheesh! Sheesh!" Look-after whispered. "Only wake when mortals make war on Faery."

"I'm not making war," Tam promised. "I've just come to see the king of the fairies, and to bring Pix back, and to take Blue back home. Blue's my baby sister, and the fairies stole her, you see, but we want her back."

The guardian peered in the pram. He and Pix pulled faces at each other. He put his hand in the pram and rubbed his fingers up and down her back, and nodded again.

"Don't you like Faery baby?" he asked, puzzled.

Tam stared at Pix. He did like her, he realized. He liked her very much now. She didn't even look very ugly in the flickery green light of the cave.

"Yes, I do like her," he said. "But she's not my sister, you see."

The guardian frowned as if Tam's answer made no sense to him. "Don't *want* her?"

Tam sighed. "I want Blue," he whispered.

Look-after growled and pulled a face at Pix, and she pulled one of her worst ones at him. Then his fingers stole towards the yellow sock, but Tam pulled it away from him.

"You can't have that," he said. "It's a
present for the king of the fairies."

"King?" The guardian glared at Tam.
He thrust his face up to him. "King far
away."

"Great-grandpa says I'll need to take Pix to the king himself." Tam could feel himself shaking now. "Please will you help me?"

The guardian grunted and shook his head. "Only prince see king," he snapped. He walked round Tam, looking him up and down. "Snee snix?" he snarled.

"Snee snix?"

The man stamped his foot. "Snee snix? Sharp silver?"

"Oh yes." Trembling, Tam lifted his sword out of the pram. "But I haven't come to make war with it. It's not sharp. It's only plastic really, and it's grey, not really silver."

But the guardian swished the sword this way and that, until it gleamed as bright as the moon in his hands. He gave it back to Tam. It was a real sword now, sharp and shining like ice, with a blue jewel set deep in the hilt.

"Snee snix splix?" he shouted. "Name him."

"Snee snix splix? Oh, what's the sword called?" Tam closed his eyes. He thought of the name of his street. "Winander," he said.

Look-after grunted. "Vinand'r, Vinand'r. Use Vinand'r well. When you see castle nightmares, snee snix, chop off heads with Vinand'r."

"Chop off their heads? I can't do that!" Tam said. "I can't chop off anyone's head!"

But the guardian just stamped his foot and hissed.

Tam put the sword back in the pram. He tried to wrap it up but the guardian whipped the dressing gown out of his hands and shook it out. It turned into a cloak of deep-red velvet. He grunted with pleasure and swung it round Tam's shoulders, so it fell in soft folds round him. Tam felt magnificent.

The guardian placed the sword Winander in Tam's belt and stood back and grinned his green teeth at him.

"Prince Tamlin," he said, bowing his head. "Welcome to Faery."

Go Wisely, Go Bravely

A voice that was not Look-after's echoed round the passage; a deep, strong, powerful voice. It came from the guardian's mouth, but it was deep and strong and frightening, not at all like his own crackly voice.

Nothing take from Faery, the voice said. *Nor food nor drink take, nor sleep have. Go wisely, go bravely, young Prince.*

Tam looked round, but there was no one to be seen but the green-haired guardian and the sleeping figures.

"How will I find the king?" Tam asked. His voice was shaking a little.

Cross the sapphire lake.

"Sapphire!" Tam said. "Like the stars!"

Do not look at your reflection. You will fall into an enchanted sleep for thousands of years. Remember this . . . remember all these things. The voice was growing fainter.

"And then what do I do, when I've crossed the lake?" Tam asked. There was no answer. "And how do I get across it? And where is it anyway?"

Silence, except for the echo of his own words. *Is it anyway? Anyway? Way?*

The guardian was watching him, arms folded, head on one side, grinning his green toothy grin. "This way, that way," he chuntered in his crotchety old voice. "Kimble."

He clicked his fingers and ambled off, and Tam followed him. It was hard work, pushing the pram over the stony ground, and he didn't want to risk waking the sleepers or making Pix cry. He followed the guardian as carefully as he could. Now he could see daylight ahead of him, and the blue gleam of water. And on the shore of the sapphire lake the old man with the green hair and beard stopped, and disappeared, just like a candle flame that has been blown out.

The Sapphire Lake

Tam gazed across the lake, almost
dazzled by its brilliance. It shimmered
ahead of him as wide and as far as his
eyes could see. There was no way
round it or over it; no shore, no bridge.
He felt like crying.

"Now what do I do?" he moaned.

Pix sat up in her pram. "Wish, wish,
a fairy wish," she whispered.

"Pix! Did you really say that? You
can talk! You can sit up already! It's
amazing!"

"Wish, wish, a fairy wish," she
whispered again.

"All right, I wish we had a boat,"
Tam said, and so it happened, just like

that, all in a moment. The pram rolled into the lake and bobbed there, big enough for two to sail in. Winander the sword became a mast, and Tam's red velvet cloak became the sail. As soon as he scrambled aboard, the little boat began to skim across the water.

Pix struggled to sit upright.

"You're too young to sit up," Tam told her, and she gurgled rudely at him. She leaned over the side, pointing down to the water and pulling faces at her reflection.

Tam stared ahead of him. He mustn't look into the lake. Whatever happened he mustn't look.

Pix started shouting and waving her arms about. She could see something in the lake past her own reflection, something wonderful and beautiful that made her face light up with smiles. She twisted her head round to look at Tam, and her eyes were shining. She looked back over the side.

"Ooh, ooh," she crooned. She laughed and sang happily. "Oooh!"

Tam so much wanted to see what she could see. Surely he could look at the lake without seeing his own face in it? Ahead of him he could see only the brilliant glitter of blue light. If he wanted to see anything else, he must look over the side of the boat.

"Oh, oh, oh!" shouted Pix.

And all round Tam hundreds of chattering voices whispered and sang, "Look and see, look and see; there is no such beauty in the mortal world. Look and see."

Tam couldn't resist it any longer. He had to look for himself. He leaned across to see what Pix could see, and at once she twisted round to him, frowning. He heard the voice that had come from the guardian in the green passage echoing round him:

Do not look at your reflection. You will fall into an enchanted sleep for thousands of years. Remember this . . .

Tam pulled himself back quickly, and the whispering voices stopped.

Now the sky and the lake had turned a much deeper blue. It began to rain. The rain turned to hail and crinkled into the bottom of the boat like little blue stones. Tam held out his hand and caught one on his palm. It lay there, not melting but glimmering with fiery blue light.

"Fairy stones. They're jewels," he said. "They must be sapphires! I wish I could show Great-grandpa! He'd know what they are."

The sapphire was beautiful. It glinted and sparkled like a tiny piece of sky.

"Take it," the singing voices chanted. "Have it. It's yours."

"Mum would love these," Tam said to Pix. "I could take her one, just this one." He closed his fingers round the sapphire.

"Yours," the voices sang on. "Yours. Yours."

Pix scrambled round to face Tam, sending the boat-pram rocking danger-ously. Water slapped over the sides. She glared at him until shivers of fear ran up and down his spine.

And the guardian voice came again:

Nothing take from Faery. Nothing take from Faery.

Tam flung the jewel as far as he could into the lake. It splashed and sank, and sent out a ring of blue ripples that spread like a peacock's tail opening out, wider and wider.

And out of the ripples rose a castle, gleaming white like snow, with golden turrets and towers, and crimson flags flying from all its pinnacles.

The Fairy Castle

The little boat-pram bumped against a shore of sparkling blue sand. Tam scrambled out and pulled it out of the water. Pix gurgled and sang and kicked her legs and flapped her arms.

"All right, all right, don't be so *impatient*," Tam said. "You were just a tiny baby when we left home. You were tiny and helpless, and now look at you. What's happening, Pix?"

He put his cloak round his shoulders and fixed Winander back into his belt, slipped the yellow sock into his pocket, and then bent down to lift Pix out of the pram. She screeched and pointed at something behind him, and he turned round to see three beasts bearing down on him, snarling and howling. They had long heads like horses and fat bodies like bulldogs. They had claws like rusty nails. They had round red eyes like flames. They had teeth like twisted spikes, and long yellow dripping tongues. One was red, one was black, and one was white. And they thundered towards the shore.

"Pix frightened," she whimpered.

"I'm a bit scared myself." Tam looked round desperately for somewhere to hide, but there was nowhere. Pix whimpered again.

✿ 58 ✿

When you see the castle nightmares, snee snix, came the voice of the guardian.

Tam felt the hilt of the fairy sword against his hand. He drew it out of his belt and swung it round in the air.

Snee snix, chop off heads with Vinand'r.

Wheesh! Wheesh! Winander sang. The nightmare beasts reared up towards Tam. He closed his eyes and gripped the hilt tightly. Wheesh! Wheesh! Wheesh! He chopped off their heads.

Tam opened his eyes and saw the three heads rolling into the lake. The black beast turned into a girl with black hair, the red beast turned into a girl with red hair, and the white beast turned into a girl with white hair. They danced round Tam.

"Thank you, thank you!" they said. "We're free! We're free!"

Tam put Winander back into his belt.

He was still shaking. "What happened?" he asked. "How did you do that?"

The girl with black hair laughed. "*You* did it! You broke the king's spell. You set us free."

"We're fairies again," the red girl sang. They opened out wings like dragon-flies, green and blue and gold, and skimmed round Tam, talking one after the other in a dizzying jumble. "But why did the king turn you into nightmares?" Tam asked. "How could he be so cruel?"

The fairy girls all spoke at once again.

"He sent us to mortal land . . ."

"Long ago . . ."

"To find what he most desired."

"But we couldn't find it . . ."

"And when we came back without it . . ."

"He was so angry with us . . ."

"That he turned us into nightmares."

"He said only a brave young prince . . ."

"From the land of mortals . . ."

"Could break the spell."

"And that was you," they finished, smiling.

"But I'm only Tam," Tam said.

"Prince Tamlin," Pix reminded him. She flapped her arms like the three fairies, then lost her balance and tumbled backwards. She stuck her thumb in her mouth and scowled.

"And now we're free!" the girls laughed. "Thank you, Prince Tamlin!" They darted away from him, over the sapphire lake. The sound of their laughter floated away like bells.

"I wonder what it was he told them

to find?" Tam said. "The king must be very, very cruel to turn them into nightmares like that. I hope he doesn't do the same to me, Pix. But I'll have to risk it, all the same. I wonder if he's in there?"

He looked up towards the castle. He could see figures on the parapets and leaning out of the towers. Three trumpets were raised – a bronze trumpet, a silver trumpet, and a golden trumpet – and they played a sweet fanfare of welcome that sounded like a forest of birdsong.

Pix raised her arms up to Tam. "Take Pix home."

The Food of Fairies

Sandy-coloured children ran towards
Tam and Pix and led them over six
stepping stones and through the castle
doorway into a courtyard. In the
middle was a fountain that showered a
plume of stars. The stars drifted down
into a pool of silver water. And there
were flowers everywhere, trees filled
with flowers, arches of flowers, lawns of
flowers. The children ran here and there
as if they were showing Pix and Tam
how beautiful it all was.

"Home! Home!" Pix struggled to be
out of Tam's arms and he set her down
gladly. She seemed to be growing
heavier and bigger by the minute. And

he had noticed something strange
about her back. Her shoulder blades
seemed to be pushing out through the
little spotted nightdress that used to
belong to Blue. And when she looked
up at him, her face was different. She'd
lost that hairy, scowly look that she
used to have.

She tried to stand up, clinging onto
his leg for support, but bumped back
down again. She flapped her
arms and grumbled. Then
she reached out to an
archway of roses and
clung onto that.
Flower petals
showered round
her and she
grabbed them
up by the
fistful and
stuffed them
in her mouth.

"Be careful," Tam warned her. "They might be full of grubs."

Pix burped and grinned up at him. Petals were stuck to her wet cheeks and her chin, clinging to her hair. She held out a fistful to him and he shook his head.

Then Tam noticed that the other children were eating flowers too, only more daintily than Pix. They wandered from flower to flower, picking a white petal here and a pink one there and smiling as if they tasted wonderful. It made his stomach growl to watch them. A girl with deep purple-coloured eyes ran over to him, holding out a wooden bowl full of petals.

"Welcome!" she said. "Are you hungry? Nectarine flowers, orange blossom, cherry. Eat, Prince Tamlin." She shook the bowl and the petals turned into gossamer froth that looked like candyfloss and smelled as sweet as strawberries.

A boy came with a crystal goblet of
petals, and when he shook it the petals
turned into sparkling liquid like
lemonade. He held it out to Tam,
nodding at him to take it. Tam was so
hungry now that he felt weak. His
throat was dry with thirst. The first girl
dipped a chocolate twig into the bowl
and put it to his lips. Tam closed his
mouth firmly and shook his head.

"Mustn't!" he said, but oh! he was dizzy with hunger. The children clustered round him with their bowls of delicious-smelling petals. "Just one, just one," they whispered. The purple-eyed girl held out the chocolatey twig again, and now it was so close to his face that he could almost taste the smell. He covered his mouth with his hand, and a voice from nowhere boomed out:

Nor food nor drink take.

Startled, the children sprang away from Tam, looking this way and that to see where the voice was coming from.

"He can see us!" the purple-eyed girl said. "He knows!"

"Who?" Tam asked. "Is it the king?"

And as if he had said the most frightening word that could be imagined, the children dropped their bowls and petals and covered their faces with their hands. And the strange

thing was, Tam's hunger and thirst had
completely gone.

He turned round to look for Pix,
and saw that she had curled herself up
on the grass and fallen asleep. Some of
the other children were
sleeping too, or
yawning, or
rubbing their
eyes. The air
was hot and

sweet with the scent of flowers. Tam
could hardly keep his eyes open. He
was drowsy with the dazzle of sunlight
and flowers, and all round him he
could hear the steady breathing of
sleeping children as one after another
they sank to their knees and curled up
on the grass. He yawned, and yawned
again. "Mustn't sleep, must stay awake,"
he yawned. His head was so muzzy
that he couldn't remember any more
why he had to stay awake.

Two of the children came to him and took his hands. They led him to a hammock made of flowers and stitched with daisy chains. He allowed himself to be lifted onto it and rocked gently, backwards and forwards, backwards and forwards. "Sleep, Prince Tamlin. Sleep," they sang, and their voices were so soft and sweet that all he wanted to do was to close his eyes, close his eyes, close his . . . close . . . cl . . .

The Starburster Is Stolen

"No! I mustn't!"

He opened his eyes as wide as he could and stared around.

Nor sleep in Faery have.

"No, I didn't, I wasn't, I wouldn't," Tam stuttered.

But he was the only one to hear the voice this time. All the children were awake now, playing a game of some kind, throwing something in the air, laughing and squealing. Pix was running across the grass towards him, shouting to him to come.

"Look! See!" she called. "Look, Prince Tamlin, look!"

The girl with purple eyes laughed

across at Tam and threw something. She caught the thing that they were playing with and threw it up in the air again, and now Tam could see something yellow slipping away from it and falling to the ground, and the tube that was inside it gleaming as it rose out of her hands.

"Hey! That's my starburster!" Tam shouted. He struggled out of the hammock and ran to a golden-haired boy who had caught the starburster, but as soon as Tam reached him the boy opened out his wings and skimmed away. He passed it to another child, who passed it to another, and Tam ran helplessly from one to the other, jumping and skipping to try to keep up. The purple-eyed girl caught it just as he reached her. She flew up above his head, tossing the kaleidoscope from one hand to the other like a juggling stick, teasing him. Then she flew to a

tree by the pool and hung upside down
from one of the branches. She dangled
there, just out of his reach.

"Please give it back to me!" Tam begged. "I must have it. It's a present for the king of the fairies."

A hush of wonder fell over the children.

"The king!" The girl in the tree gasped. "You're going to see the king!"

"Some fairies stole my baby sister and left Pix instead," Tam said. "So I've brought Pix back, and now I want Blue. And Great-grandpa said I have to give the starburster to the king. Please, please give it back to me."

"You must be very brave, if you're going to see the king," one of the boys said. "Give him his starburster, Elfa."

"Here," Elfa said. "Take it." She let the kaleidoscope slip out of her fingers, but it caught on one of the branches and bounced off as Tam ran to catch it. It fell into the pool with a splash of rainbow light, and sank to the bottom, out of sight.

Tanta

Tam stared at the pool. He couldn't believe what had happened. Pix put her hand in his and let out a howl of rage.

"What's happening out here?" A woman came running towards them, her golden hair and yellow gown billowing round her.

"Tanta! Tanta's coming!" Elfa flew down from her tree and ran to join the other children. They stood holding hands, quiet and still. One of the boys made a bubbling noise as if he were trying to keep his giggles inside himself.

The woman stopped and looked down at Tam. Her hair was as bright as sunshine around her face, and her eyes were like silver moons. Tam thought she was more beautiful than anyone he had ever seen.

"Are you the queen of the fairies?" he asked.

The children squawked and giggled, and the woman glared at them until they fell silent again. Then she turned back to Tam.

"I am not the queen of the fairies," she said. "I am Tanta! And who are you?"

"Tam," he whispered, all his courage gone.

"Prince Tamlin," Pix mumbled. She gripped his hand tightly.

Tanta looked down at Pix and plucked at her grubby nightdress. She turned her round and felt the knobbly shoulder blades. "I've never seen you before. You don't belong here."

"I do! I do!" Pix sobbed. She held out her arms to Tam and he picked her up. She put her arms round his neck and he hugged her tightly. His throat hurt so much that he could hardly speak.

"I've come all this way to bring Pix back," he said. "I walked through the green passage and I didn't wake the sleepers up. I sailed across the sapphire lake and I didn't take anything. I didn't look at my face in the water. I chopped off the heads of the nightmares and turned them back into fairies. I didn't eat when I was hungry. I didn't drink when I was thirsty. I didn't fall asleep when I was tired. I did all that so I could bring Pix home to Faery and so I could find my baby sister and take her back to Mum. But I have to give my favourite thing to the king, and I haven't got it any more."

Tanta stood with her arms folded, nodding her head. "I believe all that," she said. "You look like a brave boy who could do all that. And what is this favourite thing that you were going to give to the king of the fairies?"

"It's my starburster. It's like magic but it isn't really, Great-grandpa says. It's just clever and beautiful." Tam swallowed hard. "And it's gone."

"Gone where?"

Tam couldn't say any more. It was all too much. He stared at the pool and tears trickled down his cheeks. The fairy children gasped in horror and clustered round him, stroking his cheeks, patting him, whispering, "Don't break, Prince Tamlin. Don't break."

"Now stop that," said Tanta. "It's too sad."

Then she did an amazing thing. She stood on the edge of the pool and dived into it, and as she dived she turned into a golden fish. Seconds later she came up out of the pool in a ring of ripples and leaped into the air like a salmon. She twisted round and became herself again, standing next to Tam, completely dry. She held the starburster in her hands.

"Can I look?" she asked.

Tam nodded. He was too surprised to speak. He had actually seen fairy magic. Wait till I tell Great-grandpa! he thought.

Tanta lifted up the kaleidoscope and peered through it. She twisted it this way and that, peering at the water and the fountain and the sky and the flowers, and it seemed as if she never wanted to stop looking through it. "Man magic!" she said softly. "How wonderful it is."

She gave it back to Tam at last and watched how carefully he snuggled it into the yellow sock. He put it into his pocket and kept his hand over it, just in case.

"Come with me to the baby glade," Tanta said. "We'll see if we can find your sister."

The Baby Glade

Tanta led Tam and Pix to a shady orchard. Dabs of sunlight filtered through the leaves of fruit trees. In the cool shadows cradles were being rocked by tall elves. They all looked alike, with pointed ears and green eyes and flowing white hair.

Most of the babies were sleeping. Some were holding their hands up towards the trees, as if they wanted to catch the dapples of sunlight and shadows. Some were playing with their toes. They made the little gurgling sounds that Pix loved to make. Some bigger babies were sitting on the grass, picking tiny flowers and sucking the petals. From time to time they flapped their arms up and down.

A very few of them had tiny buds of feathers sprouting from their shoulder blades. And there were about six who had fully grown wings that opened and shut, opened and shut like the wings of butterflies. Pix pointed to them and waved her arms up and down. They stood on the tips of their toes and rose in the air, just about leaving the ground, and landed again with a bump. They laughed with excitement.

"Very good, flightlings," Tanta said as she passed them. "Soon you'll be flying. Then you won't be in the baby glade any more."

The flightlings smiled proudly at each other.

"Why haven't you got wings?" Tam asked Tanta shyly.

"Grown-ups don't have wings. We don't need them. I lost mine a long time ago."

"Don't you mind?" Tam looked back to the children by the fountain, swooping and diving in the air like birds. How he would love to be able to do that.

"Mind?" Tanta put her head to one side and thought. "Nobody really minds growing up, Prince Tamlin. Though I must say, I loved my wings. They were golden. But as soon as I lost them, I was able to shape-change, and that's very useful."

"Is that how you turned into a salmon? What else can you do?"

"That's my secret," Tanta said. "And I never, never shape-change unless it's really important. If I did it just for fun the king would make me stay that shape for ever."

"Like pulling faces? Great-grandpa says that if the wind changes when I'm pulling a face, I'll stay like that."

"Exactly. He sounds very wise, your great-grandpa. Now, have a look in the cradles and see if you can find your sister. They don't have wing-stumps when they're very small, so I really wouldn't know a fairy baby from a mortal baby."

"Mortal babies are prettier," Tam wanted to say, but didn't. He looked at Pix. She really was very pretty now she was back in Faery. Even Mum would like her.

He went from cradle to cradle and peered inside every one. He didn't have to look for wing-stubs to know that they were all fairies. Blue definitely wasn't there. When he came to the last cradle he felt like crying again.

"Are there any more baby glades?" he pleaded. "She must be somewhere else."

Tanta shook her head. "All the babies are brought here as soon as they're born, and they stay with me till they can fly. I'm sorry, Prince Tamlin. There are no more babies in the whole of Faery."

Keekwee Baba

One of the elves had been holding Pix
while Tam looked into the cradles. He
came over now and said something in
a strange language to Tanta.

"Keekwee baba?"

"Keekwee baba?" Tanta looked
shocked. The elf pulled his ears and
rocked his head from side to side.

Tanta turned back to Tam. "Morva
says there is one more baby in Faery.
But she's not your sister. She can't be."

Tam's heart rose. There was a
chance; surely there was a chance.
"Can I see her?"

"She's far away from here," Tanta
said. "And she belongs to Keekwee.

That's what the elves call the king and queen. You're not going to tell me that the queen would steal a human baby and bring her up as a fairy, are you?" She stood with her hands on her hips, glaring down at Tam. "If anyone even dared to suggest it the king would turn them into tadpoles, or something much worse."

But Tam was already moving away. "Tell me where they live. I'm going to have a look."

"You'll never find your way there on your own," Tanta called after him. "They're in their secret tower. No one is allowed to go there unless they're sent for. Hardly anyone in Faery knows the way there. Even I don't."

The elf pulled his ears again and spoke in his quick, light voice. "Emba fost ni glaz pintos."

"Morva says it's somewhere over there, past the emerald forest, up in the crystal mountains." Tanta pointed to shimmering icy mountains in the distance. "That's all he knows."

"I'll find it," said Tam. He took Pix out of the elf's arms. "I'll get there."

"Don't even try," Tanta insisted. "It's too far for you to walk, Prince Tamlin. You're only a child."

"It doesn't matter. I'll get there, however long it takes. I'm not going home without Blue," Tam said. He was scared and worried and excited, all at the same time. "Come on, Pix."

He started off out of the baby glade again, in the direction of the distant crystal mountains. They seemed so far away, and so high, and so icy, that he had no idea how he was going to do it. And when he did get to the secret tower, he had the wicked king of the fairies to face.

"It seems so impossible," he whispered to Pix. "But we've got to do it."

And Pix whispered back, "Wish, wish, a fairy wish."

"A fairy wish!" sighed Tam. "How I wish a fairy would help me!"

Pix squirmed in his arms, pointing excitedly over his shoulder. Tam turned round, and saw the most wonderful thing. Tanta had gone, and a horse was trotting towards them; a beautiful white horse with silver eyes like moons and a long flowing golden mane.

"Tanta?" Tam said.

The horse stopped by him. "Yes," she said, in a snorty, horsey voice.

The elf ran up to him and took Pix out of his arms, and Tam climbed onto Tanta's back. They set off, with Morva running in front of them, leading the way to the secret tower.

The Secret Tower

It was a long way. The emerald forest
was deep and dark. The trees stretched
out long fingers and pulled Tam
forwards and backwards and sideways
and nearly upside down. They plucked
at his cloak, they scratched his cheeks,
they pulled his hair. He could hear Pix
whimpering with fright. Morva held
her up to Tam and he leaned down
and took her. The little elf tumbled
head over heels with relief. Pix was
getting much too heavy to be carried.

Tam clicked his tongue. "On, on,
Tanta," he urged. He rode with one
arm round Pix, and his free hand
grasping Tanta's mane, while Morva

ran ahead. It was better that way, and it was comforting for Tam to have Pix with him. She chuntered happily into his ear, chewing it from time to time.

When they came out of the emerald forest at last, the crystal mountains reared above them, shiny and smooth as glass, cold as ice. Morva took Pix for a while so Tam could rest his arms, then passed her back as they started to climb the mountain. Tanta's hooves slipped and slithered. Tam was jerked backwards and forwards, but he clung onto Pix and he hung onto the golden mane. He clicked his tongue.

"On, on, Tanta," he urged.

And at last they could see the tower, as white as ice. Wispy clouds like veils swirled round it. Huge white birds with trailing feathers and piercing golden eyes swooped in and out of the mist.

"Keekwee tower!" Morva squatted on the ground with his legs crossed. He was trembling uncontrollably. He put his hands over his eyes as if he were trying to hide.

Tanta stopped. "I daren't go any further, Prince Tamlin," she said. "If the king sees me he'll make me stay a horse for ever. He might even turn me into a nightmare."

Tam slid down from her back, still clutching Pix, who was fast asleep. "Thank you for bringing me," he said. He couldn't take his eyes off the tower.

"Goodbye, Prince Tamlin. Good luck," Tanta said.

The last slope leading up to the tower was steep and slippery. Tam walked more and more slowly. He was shaking, but he didn't know whether it was with fear or tiredness. A flight of glass steps led up to the entrance, but he could hardly lift his legs to climb them. He gazed up at the tower in despair.

"I mustn't give up now, I mustn't give up now," he kept saying to himself. He put Pix down and she woke up immediately. She tried to stand up, wriggling her back from time to time as though her shoulders were itchy. There was a sudden tearing sound, and her grubby nightie ripped in two places. The feathery tips of little wings poked through the holes.

"Pix! You're nearly a flightling!" Tam said.

"I know! I know!" She beamed up at him. "Can you see them? Can you see my wings?" Her tiny feathery wings opened up like daisies, then closed again.

But she still couldn't walk, and she still couldn't fly. Tam lifted her up again and staggered up the last few steps with her. He put her down by the amber door at the entrance to the tower.

"I can't carry you any further," he panted. "You stay there and practise opening your wings. I'm going in on my own."

Blue Is Found

The inside of the tower was filled with golden light. Someone was singing a lullaby in a low, rich, beautiful voice that made Tam long to lie down and go to sleep.

"But I mustn't," he told himself. "I mustn't go to sleep. I must find Blue. I must find Blue."

The singing was coming from the centre of the golden light. It nearly dazzled him, but he shielded his eyes with his hand and crept as close as he dared. And it was as if he were walking through a wall of light, because inside all the brightness everything was dim and soft, like the glow of candles. A

woman with long dark hair the colour
of damsons was lying in a hammock
made of silvery spider webs. She wore a
skirt of grass-green silk, and yellow
satin shoes. She had a sleeping baby in
her arms and she was singing to it.

She seemed not to know that Tam was there. He tiptoed closer still, and closer. He was sure – he was so sure – that the baby was Blue.

The woman's singing grew fainter and slower. Tam could see that she was falling asleep. At last the singing stopped. The rocking stopped. The hammock stopped swinging. The fairy woman was fast asleep. Tam took a deep, slow breath and stepped forward. One pace. Two paces. Three paces. So near, and now he could see the baby's face. It *was*. It was Blue.

Tam reached forward and touched the baby's cheek, very gently. She opened her eyes at once and stared at him with wonder. Then he put his hands under her and lifted her out of the fairy queen's arms.

"Stop!" A voice like thunder echoed round the tower. Sapphire-blue lights flashed around Tam. He clutched Blue

close to him and tried to run through
the outer ring of dazzling light towards
the amber
door. Now he
could see that
the blue lights
were spiders,
dipping and
bobbing down
towards him on
silky strands.

They danced round him, spinning their threads until they wrapped him so tightly that he couldn't move his arms or his legs.

And there in front of him, brighter than any light, was the king of the fairies. He was dressed in a long tunic of white linen. He had wild silver hair like a crown of dandelion fluff, and his eyes were golden and piercing. And he was furious. He raised both his fists above his head and strode towards Tam.

"How dare you come to Faery, mortal boy?" the king roared. "How dare you enter my secret tower? And how dare you steal my baby daughter?"

The King of the Fairies

Tam struggled helplessly in his gossamer bindings. If only he could get his right hand free, he could pull his sword Winander out of his belt and chop through the spider strands. But there was nothing he could do to free himself.

The queen was awake now. She came running to stand at the king's side. She stared at Tam.

"He's only a child," she said. "Don't bind him so tight."

The king snapped his fingers and the web bindings fell away from Tam as if they were strands of hair. The queen tried to take Blue out of Tam's arms but he clung tightly to the baby. She snuffled and chuckled into his ear.

"Don't try to run away with her," the king said, "or I will turn you to stone for ever." He smiled at the queen. "He would make a pretty statue for your rose garden."

"Who are you, and what are you doing here?" the queen asked Tam.

"And don't lie," the king said. "Fairies hate lies! I can read lies, and I can read the truth. If you lie, my spiders will bind you again." The spiders bobbed round Tam on their long threads. Their jewel eyes glistened.

"I'm Tam. The fairies call me Prince Tamlin." His voice was tiny and shaky, but as soon as he spoke, the spiders ate up their threads and bobbed back up towards the hazy ceiling of the tower.

"Prince Tamlin," the king repeated, with a mocking smile. "Well, you have your velvet cloak and your silver sword. I suppose you must be a prince. And what are you doing here, Prince Tamlin?"

Tam breathed deeply to find the courage to speak again. "You stole Blue away from us, but we want her back."

"How dare you accuse us of stealing!" the king roared.

"Fairies never steal," screamed the queen into Tam's face. "Fairies take what they want, but we always leave a gift behind."

"What we want, we always get," said the king. "Always. But our servants will have left you something in exchange." He stamped his foot. "We never steal."

Tam shouted back at him, "But you never even asked us! You're wicked and cruel!" He closed his eyes. *Now* what had he done? "Why did you take our baby?" he whispered.

The queen stroked Blue's hand, and her voice became soft and sweet again. "I like mortal babies. My servants did well to choose this one. She will have a beautiful life here with us." She peered at Tam. "You could stay too."

Tam shook his head fiercely. He was too scared to speak now. He looked up at the spiders, and they peered down at him with eyes like black jet. The king walked round and round him in silence.

"I can see he's a brave boy," he said at last. "But he won't do for Faery." He snapped his fingers in Tam's face. "Go away. Go home. I won't punish you for coming. Leave the baby, and go home safely to the land of mortals."

"No," said Tam. He could feel Blue's soft breath against his cheek. "I came all this way. I came through the green passage without waking the sleepers up. I crossed the sapphire lake and I didn't look into it. I chopped off the heads of the nightmares. I did all these things so I could find Blue again and take her home. And I won't go home without her. I won't. I won't."

Again the queen tried to take Blue out of his arms, and again Blue and Tam clung to each other.

"I brought the fairy baby with me," Tam said. "She's called Pix. She can talk already. She's prettier than she used to be. She's very nice, but we didn't want her. We wanted our own baby. And I carried her most of the way here because she can't walk and she can't fly. She's very heavy, but I didn't drop her and I didn't leave her behind."

"And tell me," said the king suddenly. "How did you find my secret tower? How did you get here?"

Tam hesitated. The spiders began to bob down towards him again.

"I came through the emerald forest and over the crystal mountains," he said.

"On your own?" The king's golden eyes seemed to look right into Tam's mind.

Tam was cold with fear. If he lied, then the spiders would spin their threads round him again and he would never be free; he would never go home. But if he told the truth, Tanta and Morva would be punished. They would be turned into nightmares. He had no idea what to say.

The Starburster

"Whee! Look at Pix!" There was a sudden excited shout and a bundle of feathers shot through the amber doorway and came hurtling into the tower. "Pix can fly!" she shouted, swooping round them, her starry wings spangling in the light. "Whee!"

The king and queen ducked as she whizzed over their heads. She skidded to a halt at their feet, stray feathers floating round her, and beamed up at Tam. She closed her wings and gasped for breath. "I'm a real fairy now!"

She fluttered her wings open and took off again, just missing the king. The queen laughed and caught her.

"Not so fast!" she said. "You'll break your wings if you go as fast as that!" Pix landed again.

"I'll show you," the queen said. She lifted her arms as if they were wings and moved them slowly and gracefully up and down. "Like this."

"This is Pix," Tam said. "Your servants left her behind in exchange for Blue. *She* can be your daughter."

"Yes, please!" said Pix. She smiled her best smile and fluttered her wings.

"She's very pretty," the queen said.

"And her wings are beautiful," the king said.

It was then that Tam knew that it was quite safe for him to put Blue down and rest his arms for a bit. Nobody was going to snatch her away. The king and queen were far too busy admiring Pix's starry wings. And just as he put Blue down in the hammock, Pix flew over to him and whispered, "Don't forget the special thing!" She whizzed away again, humming happily.

"The special thing! I nearly forgot!" Tam ran to the king. "I've brought you something in exchange for Blue! I've brought you a present," he said. He put his hand in his pocket and pulled out Great-grandpa's yellow sock.

"Thank you," said the king, not taking his eyes off Pix.

"It's not the sock," Tam explained. "It's what's inside it that's special."

"Thank you," the king said again. He put his hand inside the sock and pulled out the kaleidoscope. His face lit up with surprise and pleasure. "I've seen one of these before!" he shouted. "Look! Look at my present! It's a . . . it's a . . . "

"It's a starburster," Tam said. "At least, that's what Great-grandpa calls it. You put it up to your eye and look through it."

"And you twist it this way, and you twist it that way," the king said, looking through it.

"The other end," Tam said, and turned it the right way round for him.

"Oh, man magic!" the king breathed, peering through the kaleidoscope. He danced on the tips of his toes with excitement. "Nothing in Faery is as wonderful as this. Oh, I've always wanted one of these." He walked around with it, peering at everything – at his feet, at the queen, at Pix's wings, at his spiders – and every new thing he looked at made him gasp and laugh out loud. "My word!" he said.

"That's what Great-grandpa says."

"I saw a little boy looking through one of these once," the king said, still not taking the kaleidoscope away from his eye. "It was in mortal land, and it was just outside the green passage. He was looking through a . . . a starburster just like this and he kept saying, *My word! My word!* Oh, I so much wanted to see what he could see! I looked through the other end and he looked straight at me! And he shouted out loud, *My word! A fairy!*"

Tam felt a great bubble of excitement inside him. "I know who it was! Was it about ninety years ago?"

"I think it was yesterday," the king said. He took the kaleidoscope away from his eye for just a second. "But time is different in Faery. Actually, Prince Tamlin, he looked a bit like you."

Home

The king and queen and Pix spent a long time looking through the kaleido-scope and laughing and exclaiming, "My word!" at every new thing they saw. Tam rocked Blue in the hammock, watching them, and as soon as she woke up he lifted her out and said, "If you don't mind, I think we'd better go now."

"Of course," said the king. He looked surprised, as if he had forgotten all about Tam. "Any time. I'll send for someone to show you the way. They'll be at the bottom of the glass steps."

"Thank you for bringing our fairy child back," said the queen. "Your sister is very nice, but I really think I like Pix better."

Pix flew up to Tam. She landed daintily and smiled up at him. "Goodbye, Prince Tamlin. Thank you for looking after me." She fluttered her wings for him.

"It's all right, Pix," he said. His voice was husky. "Take care now." He couldn't bring himself to say goodbye, but walked slowly through the dazzling light and out through the amber archway.

And there, waiting for him at the bottom of the glass steps, were a white horse with a long flowing golden mane and silver eyes, and an elf with green hair and pointed ears.

"Tanta and Morva! You're still here!" Tam ran down the steps. Morva helped him onto Tanta's back and handed Blue back up to him, and they were off, galloping like the wind, over the crystal mountains, through the emerald forest, and they came to the white castle.

"Off you get," said Tanta. "We can't take you any further."

Tam handed Blue down to Morva and slid off Tanta's back, and when he

❄115❄

turned round the horse had gone, and
there was golden-haired Tanta again,
smiling at him and rocking Blue in
her arms.

"Mortal babies are very beautiful!"
she sighed. "No wonder the king and
queen wanted one. And no wonder
your mother wants her back. There's
your boat, waiting for you."

Sure enough, there was the little
pram-boat on the blue sand. Morva
helped Tam to push it into the water.
He bowed to Tam and then clasped
both his hands in his own.

"Far good Tamlinkee," he said. "Far good baba."

"Far good Morva," said Tam. He climbed into the boat.

Tanta handed Blue down to Tam and pushed the boat gently away from the shore. She clapped her hands.

"Goodbye, Prince Tamlin," she called. "Goodbye, Baby Blue."

The pram-boat scudded across the sapphire lake with Winander for a mast and the velvet cloak for a sail, and in no time at all they had reached the other side. Tam pulled it out of the water and it became a pram again.

"Nearly there, Baby Blue," he said, and she gurgled sleepily at him. He trundled her over the rocky ground into the dark tunnel. A flickering light came towards him. Now he could see old Look-after, with the green hair and the long green beard. The old elf came straight up to the pram and peered inside. He grinned his green toothy grin, and pointed a bony finger at Blue. She curled her own fingers round it and hiccuped.

"Splix?" Look-after asked.

"Splix? Oh, her name! She's called Blue. My baby sister Blue," Tam said proudly.

"Baba satta Blue," said Look-after softly.

Then he jerked his head and led Tam past the sleeping guardians to the dark cave. He bowed.

"Goodbye, Prince Tamlin!"

Tam paused for a moment. He could still hear Pix's voice, as clear as anything, laughing and singing far away. He could hear the queen and king of the fairies, he could hear Elfa and the other sandy-coloured children, and Tanta and Morva, and then all the voices faded away. Tam felt his cloak

slipping away from his shoulders and
Winander sliding out of his belt. He
looked down and saw his dressing-
gown and plastic toy sword on the
stony ground, and bent down to pick
them up. And just as he put them at
the bottom of Blue's pram two huge
boulders at the end of the cave rolled
apart, and daylight flooded through.

He pushed the pram down the green
passage. The boulders rolled to behind
him, and there sitting on the grass in
front of him were Mum and Dad and
Great-grandpa, eating sandwiches and
drinking lemonade.

"My word," said Great-grandpa. "It's our Tam."

"Just in time for the picnic," said Dad.

And Tam lifted Blue out of the pram and put her, safe and sound, into Mum's arms.